Marina Peters

Too Deep In With The Auditor

A Martin Muller Audit #1

Too Deep In With The Auditor

A Steamy Romance Novel

By

Marina Peters

marinapetersbooks.com

Impressum

Bibliografische Information der Deutschen Nationalbibliothek:
Die Deutsche Nationalbibliothek verzeichnet diese Publikation in der Deutschen Nationalbibliografie; detaillierte bibliografische Daten sind im Internet über http://dnb.dnb.de abrufbar.

© 2020 Marina Peters
Herstellung und Verlag: BoD – Books on Demand, Norderstedt
ISBN: 978-3-7504-6997-6

TOO DEEP IN WITH THE AUDITOR

There it is. The email that's going to ruin my weekend. How do I know? It's from Dick. He never sends me anything, certainly not a meeting request on Friday at 3 pm for 4:30 pm. I took a second and thought if I should just duck out. But that would just leave me hating him until Monday. Might be worth it? But he didn't give me a chance. Next thing I know he's at my door.

"Hey, Martin. I have a thing at 4:30 with the wife."

"Want to reschedule Dick?" I asked and watched him twist his face. His name is Richard and he hates when I call him Dick. Could just be the way I emphasis it thought.

"Ok. Well, I need you out on an audit pronto," he said with a little shitty smile.

"Pronto?"

"Yeah, you need to be on site by Monday."

"Fuck me. Monday?"

"Bank of Herrin in Carterville. Found some little branch that fell through the cracks."

That was Donald's audit. he had two crews out there already. The bank had a pile of small branches whose records were only partly computerized.

"I have no one else to send. And I know I need someone fast and efficient."

"No can do Dick. There are IT considerations, as well as accommodations and all the prep," I told him.

"That's why I am sending Jen with you and I gave Ops a call already, they should be working on that, have a good week," He said. No wonder he was smiling he was screwing me hard without lube.

"Week?"

"We need it in a week, to marry up to Donald's part. It's a small branch. But we need a one-man wrecking crew, and that's you. Unless…"

"No. Fuck. I'm going."

"Good see you in a week."

This is BS and he knows it. I think this has more to do with the New York Senior partners meeting. I would not be able to go and that would fuck me out of a promotion for another year.

They could have just as easily filed for an extension. But knowing Donald that was probably already done and they are out of time. So it's off to Podunk financial I guess. I need to make a few calls and let down a few choices and sexy women I planned to get to know inside and out. But that would have to wait now.

+Jen and Martin

I was handling the last of my calls when Jen came in and sat down. She was a funny little thing. All of five feet. A little a cup stick girl, and a lot of goth. She had a pile of violet tribal tattoos and some blood red roses and skulls. The Mexican sugar skull kind. She would have red hair if she didn't die it black. She tended to wear black jeans and a black tee-shirt with black combat boots. You get the idea. She was quick and wicked smart with computers. In it, she was the one-woman wrecking crew.

"Jen, what can I do you for?"

"Hey, boss. I hear that we are headed south."

"Yeah. I can hear the banjos playing now."

"Not that far south."

"Just about, you up for physical security assessments? I don't think IT is their strong suit."

"Herrin? They have most of the last five years on the system. They are scanning the rest and bringing up a gigabit dedicated fiber line. But yeah I have my camera and old-timey typewriter too," she said.

I had to laugh. She was a riot on the Bank of Florida audit too. She loved the numbers as much as I did and she loved a challenge. Some people think auditing isn't sexy but they just don't know. Jen did.

"So, Carterville?" She asked.

"No, much worse. Cambria, even smaller. Can you drive an RV?"

"What?"

"You know. One of those big sexy motor homes?" I asked. I was kidding but by the looks of the selection of two and three-star hotels a viable option.

"Well, yes," she said. "My dad and I used to drive to Pennsylvania every Christmas and there would never be enough room in my aunt's house so, Yeah. He taught me to drive one." Great, now I have to get an RV.

"You're shitting me? Why does that not surprise me?" I said.

"So. That means you want me to ride with you then?"

"I'll talk to ops, text you were to meet me. We are taking off in the morning. I can at least squeeze in a night with Inga," I said. Jen smiled at me and may possibly be gotten a little bit pink in color.

+Ops and Martin

I emailed heather in ops and asked if she could get an RV. Then I looked around for a nice restaurant to take Inga. If I was going to get lucky I had a limited time to impress her and seal that deal. Heather appeared at my door.

"What do you mean an RV martin? Why not a Hotel?" She asked. "Where the fuck am I supposed to get an RV?"

"Hotel, that would good. Think Motel and Bedbugs. Have you seen the motels? The only place they have five stars there is in the sky. I would get a room but then I would have to set it on fire," I said only half-joking. I picked up my briefcase and finished loading my USB memory stick up for the trip.

"Fine. But you owe me, I want the 1976 Pinot. For my dad's birthday."

"What? This is not a favor, it's your job."

"And you want me to find you an R-fucking-V on Friday at 4. No, I could just set a motel and send you with some Ridit and Calamine."

"Ok, Ok. Fine. Thanks, Heather."

"Have a good week Martin."

"Sure. Everyone keeps saying it, won't make it true."

I pulled the USB stick out of the computer and put it in my pocket and grabbed my briefcase. "Text or email me the details."

+++

I felt like a convict walking the green mile. Well, at least I will get a model and a lobster for my last meal. I was almost to the elevator bank and I spotted her. Five-foot nine of trouble. Mrs. Dick. We have a sort of love-hate thing going. Mr. Richard Franklin, her husband hates me, and Mrs. Eloise Franklin loves me. Which is probably why Dick hates me.

Now that I come to think of it. Probably why he does not want me going to New York. It will keep her on his arm instead of hob-nobbing with me.

"Martin. How have you been? I have plans for New York," she said in a low sultry tone.

"Eloise. Always a vision. Sorry to disappoint, but your husband just sent me on an emergency audit." I pressed the elevator button.

"You're serious? Is there even such a thing?"

"The devil is always looking for his due."

I saw Dick walking toward us when the elevator opened and Eloise grabbed my arm and pulled me in. She pressed the close door button hard and often. As I pressed the lobby button. Dick hurried over just in time to see her smile at him and the door close.

"You trying to get me fired Eloise?"

"No, I'm trying to get laid," she said and pressed herself into me. Good god, she had a body and she was willing. But my flesh was weak and I had a time table to keep.

"No can do."

"Not you jackass," she tapped the side of my face in a playful slap. and laughed. "Richard."

"Ok, I'll bite, what are you talking about."

"He will be on fire now wondering where I went. What I am doing and to whom I am doing it. I'll go to the spa for a couple of hours and come home all steamy and having just taken a hot shower. He can smell that one me."

"You're a monster, you know that?"

"Maybe, I took your advice after that Christmas party when he thought we screwed he turned into an animal."

"Great."

"He will want to fuck the hell out of me and take me anywhere I want to go for dinner."

The elevator hit the lobby and she gave me a peck on the cheek and hopped out and walked out. Dick was a lucky man, luckier still that she put up with his ass. I headed for the parking garage. Hot models wait for no man, not for long.

+Jen

Heather needed to find an RV and wondered where you even get one. Just then Jen walked by with her normal slouch and deep introspective look as she read some binder.

"So, I hear your headed south with Martin?" She winked at Jen.

"It's no big deal, a week on-site, looking at their stuff. routine."

"Routine?"

"Yeah, what is that supposed to mean?"

"Your blushing and well, Martin and you on the road." Heather raised her eyebrow a little.

"Please I have a boyfriend if anything this is awkward for me," Jen said.

The awkward was right, the boyfriend was a fantasy. Heather knew the guys in IT were still grappling with how to ask Jen out. Nerd mating was a complex ritual of accidental courting.

"Hey, help me out here. You got any idea where to get an RV."

"Yeah. RV America, it's online."

"Cool thanks."

Finally free of heather Jen walked quickly away. She didn't like small talk or hanging with the girls. She did have a thing for Martin and she was pretty sure she had been to bed with him. Thing is, she couldn't remember because she got pretty blotted at the after-party for the audit. it's not like she had not done something like

8

that before. She had the Video to prove it. Girls on spring break 3, in all her glory and a few guys to boot. Jen had bought several copies thinking that each one she bought would be one someone wouldn't have access to. She had almost made it when heather called after her. "Have a good week." Jen needed to go to the gym and work out, then take a cold shower. This was going to suck.

+Martin

The address was a little out of the way and in an industrial district. I unpacked my two suitcases and the guy took me to the RV. It was massive, one of those tour bus looking types and the inside was really nice. Two pull-outs. Jen should have been here a while ago. I checked my phone and tried to call. But it went straight to voice mail.

"So. Just have to check your license," He said.

"Sure OK." I handed him my driver's license.

"This won't work I need to see your class A or a Class A non-commercial endorsement."

"What? Your kidding."

Finally, Jen arrived in a cab and she was fit to be tied as she pulled out her little rolling bag and a computer case as well.

"We might need to downsize. What can I drive with that?"

"This, like a 16 footer," he said.

"Sorry, I'm late. What's the deal. Whoa. This here. I have always wanted to drive on like this."

"Who's this?" The guy asked.

"My driver," I said, he looked shocked.

"Can you even reach the pedals?" He said and grinned at me. Probably not a good moment for the joke.

"Ha Ha Ha, jack ass. It's not she doesn't have hydraulics and seat adjustments," She looked him with an attitude that's all I could say. Then she reached back and got out her wallet. A black leather one on a chain.

"Nice accessory, that comes with the shoes?" I asked and she looked at me with irritation.

"Here," she said and handed the guy her wallet.

"Class A and a Class B commercial. Nice, that will do. But only you can drive," He said and wrote a few things down.

"Wait. You have the License."

"Yeah. I drove a truck when I was going to college. My dad is a truck driver. We teamed up. I told you he taught me to drive an RV. Did I not mention the trucks?"

"No. No, you did not."

"Fuck this must be 42 feet," she said.

"Forty-five, put the struts down before you do the pull-outs," The guy said, gave us a paper and we were off.

I was a little nervous when we got in and she jumped into the seat. It really did look funny. But she was right at home. She dug around and put on some glasses and started the rolling mansion up. She maneuvered the beast onto the road and onto the highway without breaking a sweat.

"This is a sweet RV. Thanks for letting me drive."

"Well you heard the man, I'm not qualified."

"Well, you will be living large? I got a room in some shitty motel down the street. I hope they heat works. I hate those bullshit things that make everything damp. And I hope the credit card holds. They are charging like 65 dollars a day for that dump."

"What, a swamp cooler? Should be fine, and what are you worried about? The firm foots the bill for these trips anyway."

"Sure for the Auditors, I have to get all my shit approved after I come back show receipts. Mr. Franklin still hasn't approved the last two trips and I need to pay my card. Minimums got to love them."

That was sort of bullshit. But it's the kind of shit Dick would pull. He seemed to like having power.

+Jen talking to Martin

Jen was looking a little more pale than usual by the time we turned into Carterville. I decided to have her pull over and we would get something to eat and then drive to the bank a few miles away.

"Wow, this is a tiny place. But it sort of reminds me of Florida."

"Sure if Florida had Snow and no nightlife. Oh and the religious nuts," I said.

"It's not so bad. You should see the town I come from. Hey, tomorrow is Sunday, want to go to church?" She said and smiled.

"Tell me your kidding."

"Well, Yeah. But hey I am a certified minister," She said as we got out.

"Of course you are."

We sat and ate and in the light of the restaurant she really did look bad. Jen did not look at all like she was going to enjoy the motel and given I had no nightlife options I thought I would invite her to stay in the RV.

"So. You looking forward to the roach motel."

"Not really," she shrugged.

"Look, that thing is huge, it's got two bedrooms. You can take the back and I'll set up the pullout in the front. There should be plenty of room."

"Oh, I couldn't do that. You take the back. I don't want to be trapped in the back when you decide to drag home some barflies," she said.

"Now how would that look? Some woman laying around in the front when I do. Besides, you said it was

13

like Florida, you were right, we had fun. But again, I haven't seen much skin since we pulled in."

"If you're sure. Yeah, OK."

She looked a little better after that. But her nose was red and she was sniffling.

'You OK."

"Allergies. I've got a serious headache too."

"Ok, well let's go park and settle in. I have a day to prep. You look like the trip kicked your ass doing all that driving."

+Ellis

With night falling on a Saturday night I had the impulse to go to the back and check up on some of the records. But I decided against it. That damn auditor was coming Monday and for what? Risk assessments? My ass, they were looking to close and consolidate. I took over as the branch manager six years ago and this was my first audit. I decided to call my friend at the main branch.

"Hey, Donna. Hows it going. Say, listen I was calling about the audit."

"That. Please I am trying to get drunk here and forget."

"That bad?"

"Worse, that guy Don is a jack ass."

"Is he coming Monday?"

"No. Some other guy is coming from the firm. Out of Chicago. He's not part of the crew I have here. He's a specialist. God's gift I guess. Some young exec."

"Great he's looking to make a name then at my expense."

"You be fine. He cannot be worse than the guy over here. It's been like a bad marriage with no sex."

It was driving me crazy. There is a lot of old records still in the vault that never got digitized two years ago. We were working on it but we were months away from finishing. I worried if we had missed anything. I decided to hop over and take a look. Not sure what I would do, but I had a day to check it out and prepare.

+Chris

The weather's been holding fine but no telling if it's going to be dry or wet these days. The cold and heat never seemed to change. Roaring down the unpaved trail looking at the farms and livestock to be sure my investments are safe. These folks mean well but they don't have the education I do. My family has owned a lot of this land for generations. Since the land rush. The rest we bought up. My father used to say "There's no equity in a plow or beast. It's getting other people to do that and you manage the land." So, that's what I do. Manage.

I pulled onto the main highway the truck flinging mud I thought I would head to the truck stop and wash her. On my way, I noticed that there were lights on at the bank. I thought an excuse to stop in and see if Ellis was in. That woman will be the death of me I swear.

I have known her for years and she loves to torture me with that body of hers. Just the best rake in the county and hips. We have been together off and on and I cannot dial that filly in. She is willful that is a fact.

The door was open, she was on the phone looking stressed. But that's her. Never known her to be stressed. Some sort of audit from what I overheard. She's not wearing a bra and has on that AC/DC t-shirt I like. Got it for her at a rodeo I took her to back ten years now. It's a schoolboy notion but I figure, she still has it, must still be a memory that she's hanging onto. I decided no harm in saying hi as she set down the phone.

"Hey, little lady. How're tricks."

"Oh fuck. I left the door unlocked. I'm fine Chris. I don't have time for you right now, what do you want."

She is a feisty, my lord. I only said hi. Would it kill her to say hello and how do you do. But this is why I planted the excuses in my head before stepping into the bank.

"Come to see about the seed loans. How we doing on that."

"What? I have staff handling that I don't know."

"Yeah, I'm working on it with the loan officer, but I don't work well with others."

So here we go, the dance is the same, I start out charming and then comes the rest.

"We are going to need collateral. Which land plots are you putting up."

"I'll get you a list. You know Ellis, would it kill you to smile. We ain't gone out in what three months. When are you gonna put the knife down?"

Then she got up. That ain't good. "Your kind of a jack ass leaning these farmers for the land and the profit of the crop."

"What? I am helping them. This is a business and they are my partners. If they lose I lose, they stay on and try again. I'm taking a risk here."

"You're a predator. Half these people have farmed and raised cattle for your family for years. And they get what? None of their kids have ever gone to college. Not one new place has been built in ten years. You know how I know that Robert?"

"I'm, sure you're going to tell me."

17

"I know that because I have had to deny fifteen loans for houses in the last ten months, they don't have the down and they will never have the downs. Never. Not on what they make with your claws into them. Say what you want, you're a predator."

"Well, the thing is, we need the apex predators, don't we. Keeps the everything healthy," I said my jaw tight. She might have all that book learning behind her from Chicago but she has no clue. I have had this economy debate before. Always ends with the word 'fair' the one thing life ain't.

"Only you could think that was a compliment, Chris."

Fuck me. Don't she have a way of making me look like an ass in the space of a single sentence. Back out at the truck, I got in. I know better. Insanity is trying the same thing and expecting a different result. I signed and started her up. I pulled away like I always seemed to, shaking my head.

+Martin

Jen was absolutely the most fascinating thing at this firm and now she's gotten even more fun. A truck driver of all things. She's more man than any man I have ever known but she's definitely a hot little number. I am speaking from the experience of watching a video of her on spring break. I found it on the internet and could not help myself. Someone in IT had said she had been to Florida before and indicated there might be some nudes of her, and that prompted me to search. We got along well and when she got drunk at the after-party I saw a half of IT moving in to get lucky, the perverts. So I took her to my room and let her sleep it off. She got pretty hot and sweaty and took off everything, I guess she sleeps nude. She was sprawled out when I got back in the morning and I covered her up. This is how I know she's a redhead and all of her tattoos. I was thinking about my missed promotion opportunity when she asked a question. It was like she read my mind.

"So you bummed about New Your?" Jen asked.

"Are you?"

"No. You know I hate those things. Besides I'm topped out. Smashed right up against that glass ceiling tight as I can go," Jen said. "To make more I need to take on a team of those nut jobs and all they do is stare at my tits. I think I am going to have to start my own company or do an app. Or marry someone on the way up and then do an app."

"And take care of babies?"

"Do I have to?"

"Generally expected of wifely duties I am told."

"Fuck. Have to rethink that plan."

Jen never liked to go to functions because, as she put it, "She didn't like to wear a bra. They weaken the muscles and make your tits sag." So that tells you a little about how she thinks. It's never quite what you imagine. Not that she and gravity were having much of a fight, but she was a comfortable smallish b or maybe a? I can never really tell. Hell, I have no idea what size my underwear is, that's the sales ladies job. But she is cute.

"Yeah, I can see that being a pain in the ass. I guess we all have our cross to bear. Pull in here. Where that truck is pulling out."

+Pulling into the bank

It's later than I wanted to be here. But it was Saturday and that fucked all to do anyway. So I figured we would just park in back and set up the RV. Maybe I could take a walk, see if there was a local watering hole to scope any action.

"Hey, there's someone at the bank. See she's locking the door."

"Must be the manager, Ellis something," I said.

"Well, she's following us," Jen said watching the side mirror.

"Good. We can ruin her weekend and introduce ourselves. The locals always hackle up when they see an auditor," I said.

"You're an asshole you know," Jen said.

"It's a gift."

+Ellis

Oh fuck me. What is this now? Some geriatric caravan that's come to spend the night at the bank. There was a young girl with Tattoos driving. I shook my head and followed it to the back. Someone was getting out and stretching.

"Excuse me, we are not an RV rest stop," I said. He was a lot less geriatric than I anticipated so it was going to be a little easier to be an asshole. He was a good looking guy. Dress comfortably but even in jeans and a T-shirt, he had that GQ look. Chiseled and confident. I had just gone around with Chris and I was in no mood.

"Yeah, I get that. I'm, Martin Muller, this is my partner Jen, she's the security consultant. We like to be close to work, no distractions he lied. It's temporary. You understand."

Well shit. This is just getting better and better. "So, you're the auditors."

"That's us," his little sidekick Jen says and eyed me. Might as well be gracious and just make the best of it.

"Ok well, then just park over there more toward the dumpsters," I said and the girl looked at them suspiciously.

"Those the dumpsters the bank disposes of papers? It has a lock." She asked with a tone.

"No, papers go to the basement, a destruction company comes in and shreds there," I responded trying to stay calm.

"Good answer, then what?" says Jen. You're kidding me right now are we comparing dick sizes. Ok little girl, let's go.

"We actually have an incinerator we use it for heat. Very green."

She didn't have any more questions.

"Done with the third degree?"

"For now," Jen said.

+Martin

Wow. Catfight. Gotta love it. I thought nothing exciting was going to happen. Ten seconds in Jen is on this woman.

"Good Answer?" I said to Jen. "And we are worried about me being an asshole."

"What? Don't think I am not going to go look in those cans."

"Down girl, can you handle the setup. I want to see if there is a store," I said.

"Yeah. And see if they have a bar too," Jen said. I looked at her sideways.

"What? I know that's what you're going to do anyway. Might as well give you permission to disappear," she said.

+Jen

As I watched Martin walk away I couldn't help but think how his eyes have been glued to the manager the bank. She was so hot, those have to be D sized hits and Martin is definitely a tit man. And look her walk Jesus she has legs for days and those hips.

Against womanlike, I have no chance, zero. Thank God.

In a way, I have sort of a home-court advantage. As if Martin would ever even look at me.

Sunday

+Martin

Saturday night in Cambria was about what I expected. It was a quiet and sleepy town and went to bed pretty much at five. There was a little bar but I didn't really feel like drinking after driving all day. I stopped by a small convenience store picked up a few beers some chips and a couple of candy bars to stock up. Then I headed back.

Jen had finished setting up all the pullouts and was already asleep when I got back to the trailer. So I opened a beer sat back and watched some Netflix on my laptop. As happens most days I fell asleep watching some movie and woke up bright and early Sunday morning as Jen came bumping through the kitchen wearing very little.

"You look a little hot," I said.

"Thanks," Jen replied with a smile. But she had a red nose and immediately sneezed.

"No, like, hot hot. Are you sick?"

"It's a little cold maybe, I guess it started coming on Friday."

"I guess no church for you today. You better not get me sick that's just going to make the weak hell."

"I'll be fine. It's a small bank the assessment should only take a day."

"Well, I guess I'll go get you some Tylenol and Nyquil. I think I saw drugstore up the street."

"Don't make a fuss I'll be fine."

26

She didn't look like she was going to be fine as she plopped down on the couch and fiddled with the remote for the big screen TV that was in the RV. I noticed that Jen wasn't much for modesty. Other than A pair of booty socks and the T-shirt she was airing out all the goods.

It was pretty clear that Jen wasn't going to be up for going out for food so I drove over to Carterville to pick up some supplies. They had the right aid there so I got the necessary pharmaceuticals as well. By the time I got back, Jen was passed out on her bed again with her T-shirt around the bottom of her tits. So I decided to cover her up and put the bucket of chicken I bought into the fridge.

Sunday was going to be beyond boring, it happened that the bars were closed due to some local event. So I resigned myself to the fact that other than taking a walk I was pretty much going to be watching movies and browsing the Internet all day. Punctuated by the odd toilet flush when Jen went to the bathroom and coughing fit. I decided I needed to go back out and get about five boxes of tissues for her. This was one weekend I prayed for Monday.

+++

Thank goodness right it was still open and had a sale going on tissues. But then I wondered if we had toilet paper? So I decided to buy a 12 pack of double-ply toilet paper instead, kill two birds with one stone. As I thought about anything else we might need I spotted the bank manager coming up the aisle.

"Hey, is there anything to do in this town besides brief on Sunday," I said trying to be charming. The glare I got told me it probably didn't work.

"That's pretty much it unless you're rancher," she responded. Mostly I think to be polite.

"Oh, what happens if you're rancher?"

"Then you get to feed the cows," she said in a dry tone and started to walk by me.

"Are you mad at me for parking in your bank's parking lot? Or do you just hate auditors."

She considered her words for a moment. I suspect she was trying to filter out the bad words. "This is my first audit, so yeah it's a little unnerving. Especially since the other team hasn't really impressed us with their efficiency and competence."

"Oh yeah, that's Donald, not exactly high functioning. But that's what he sent me to do in a week what it's taken them two months to do."

"So you think you're some kind of a hotshot," she said.

"No, I don't think it all."

"Wow, must be that all men are arrogant ass holes."

I watched her walk down the aisle all business. I get it she was trying to establish who was in charge. Time to mend some fences.

"So listen you want to grab a beer."

She turned around and looked at me as though I had an ugly wart on my face.

"Did you just seriously ask me that. Even if I did think you were charming you're the auditor. I don't think that would be appropriate. And if you do that work I'll make a harassment complaint."

She had a terse little smile when she said it so I think it was a challenge. Then she turned around and kept walking. What a feisty little thing, and where there's smoke there's fire. Sunday was a bust but maybe the rest the week held some promise.

+++

When I got back Jen was in the shower. The charming set of noises, but soon I heard her blowing her nose emanating from the small stall. I wondered how much water we had available because it seemed like she was taking a long time.

"Hey save some water for the rest of us," I called out to her.

"I ran the hose over to the sprinkler system genius," she said like I was supposed to know. "Where did you go?"

"Oh, you know out to get some toilet paper. Figured you'd need something to blow your nose."

"You really are an idiot. Good thing I brought some actual facial tissue. Toilet papers way too rough."

"Whatever, how you feeling? You want something to eat?"

"I feel better since taking the Tylenol. I smelled the chicken earlier, I know it's going to taste like ass but I need to eat something."

So I heated up some chicken and turned on some Netflix. Probably the first time in my life I really did actually chill. It wasn't long before Jen fell back to sleep on my bed. So I decided better to take the master bedroom tonight and leave her where she was at.

Monday

It was definitely not a cold. It was definitely the flu. Monday morning Jen looks like death warmed over. She kept insisting she was okay but I knew better and when she almost passed out standing up I think she finally took my advice and stayed in bed.

I showered and dressed and decided against staying in the RV for breakfast. It was probably a good idea that I stay far away from Jen as possible. The bank wasn't open yet so I went down the street to a diner. I was hopeful for a young waitress but as is the case in small towns the waitress was older than I was. I think her name was Mabel and she kept calling me hon and asking me if I was still working on that.

"What times a bank open," I asked Mabel.

"Oh, I don't know maybe nine or 9:30. You want me to wonder coffee up for you again hon."

"No, I have a full day sitting in the vault at the bank. Don't want to be running to the bathroom every five minutes."

"Oh, you're the jackass. I heard about you, you're an auditor. My Leonard got audited last year and it was a horrible mess. They said we owed $5000. Now my Leonard and the smartest man in the world but that ain't right," she said

"I'm not an IRS auditor. I review the bank to make sure they're following the rules with the FDC and banking standards. Besides banks tend to have quite a bit of money. What does your Leonard do?" I asked.

"He's a mechanic. Why? What's that got to do with anything?"

By the quality of that reply, I figured Leonard was probably a real genius if she considered herself smarter. But when you're from out of town and the locals already have it in for you it's a good idea to build some goodwill.

"Well, then I bet Leonard has a bunch of deductions that he may not be aware of."

"Well he's just a shade tree mechanic, he doesn't have a shop. And the IRS didn't say anything about deductions."

"Well, they're not in the business of mentioning how not to pay taxes. I bet Leonard's tools are expensive, and he can deduct some of that. And if he works out of his garage you can deduct a percentage of your house for the business. And things like that."

"Sounds complicated. Why does it all have to be so complicated."

"Tell you what have Leonard come up in the morning to the diner and bring his tax papers for the last five years. I'll take a look at them and see what I can do."

She was beside herself when I made the offer and told me she didn't have any money. That's what I figured so I told her I would do it for free. They were just taxes and simple ones at that probably. I can't imagine Leonard made much I could probably help them in my sleep. But it was a small town and if word got around that an ass hole auditor was at the bank in less than a day then the news of the nice guy helping Leonard with his taxes would travel just as fast.

+++

But the news didn't travel fast enough. When I got to the bank there were three sets of glaring eyeballs staring back at me. I guessed a couple of tellers in the loan officer.

"Hi, I'm…"

"We know you are, our managers not in yet so you just gonna have to wait."

"Yeah, I met your manager over the weekend. I would just speed this up and you show me where the vault is so I can get started. I looked around and it didn't seem that the vault was on the ground floor." But they just blinked at me.

"Can I use this desk?"

"Suit yourself," the teller said. So I set up my laptop on the desk and started doing some preliminary work.

+++

By 1 o'clock I was done with everything that I could possibly do without access to the papers in the vault. And still no Ellis. I had worked through lunch so I thought I would get something to eat and check on Jen.

"I get something to eat. When did you say that the lease was going to be in?" I asked one of the tellers. That's when the loan officer piped in.

"Oh, she called about 9:45 and said she wasn't coming in today. Personal day. She said to give you access to the vault when you needed it."

Just great, I'd have just about enough of Monday so I decided to take the rest of the day off.

"Just tell her I'll be back tomorrow. She's going to be in tomorrow right?"

"Should be," Was all she said and turned back to whatever she was doing.

+++

I went back to the RV and found Jen had eaten all the chicken. It was still passed out. At least the bar is going to be open. So I changed my clothes and headed down the street. By the time I got there it was only 1:30 but there was already a healthy crowd of regulars. By the look and the smell of them, it seemed to be a group of ranchers. The buxom little barmaid mixing drinks behind the bar was mostly passing out beers as fast as she could open them.

"What no tap?" I asked her.

"Hi, do you look new. We used to have a tap but these Neanderthals don't really care. All we need do is carry a few thousand bottles of a couple of brands and I don't have to wash glasses."

"Efficient, what do you have besides beer?" I asked.

"Well, there's whiskey, Jack and Coke, what you want."

"Can you do a long slow screw against the wall?"

That made her smile.

"It's a long slow comfortable screw against the wall actually, and don't have Galliano."

"Oh, so you know your drinks?"

"Sure I do, got trained up in Chicago, worked there for five years I guess."

"So what brings you to this hellhole."

"You mean what brings me back. It's the same story: a boy. I went to school here couldn't wait to get out but the big city wasn't all that was cracked up to be. At the end of the day, he came up to Chicago and asked me to come back. Truthfully I was ready the big city beat me down but it worked out," She said. "You from Chicago?"

"Born and raised. Only left it for a little while to go to New York for college. So I guess you married a rancher to?"

"No, farmer."

Just then a group of rowdy men descended on the bar and ordered 20 beers which averaged out to about three each. One guy had a look like he could be a double for Sam Elliott right out of "Road House", everybody was happy to see him. I guess he was buying.

"Well, how about a Tequila Sunrise?" I asked her.

"Kind of a girl drink around here better not let anyone see you drink that."

"Well I'm trying to get in my vitamin C my business partner is sick and that's all I need."

"Wow, ever think of maybe eating an orange or balanced diet maybe take a vitamin?"

"Who's that guy looks like a cowboy, silver hair, life of the party."

"That guy? He's Chris gentry. Comes in here two or three times a week with his crew and a few farmers. They get a little rowdy and play darts. That's the thing about farmers and ranchers to get up early work hard. But they play hard too," she said.

"I can see that," I said and took my drink and sat down.

+Ellis

I have been pretty hard on Chris when he came into the bank. It beat me all Sunday, I was just wound up from that damn audit. He didn't deserve me snapping at them or calling him a predator. He was the bank's best customer and ran a lot of cash through us. He just makes me so mad. I hate it when he calls me a little lady.

I decided to take the day off and go see him at his ranch. To apologize. But when I got there he wasn't there. I guess he needed an extra hand on one of the farms and so he helped out with something. Knowing Chris it was to repair a tractor or maybe help birth a calf. He really was a good guy if he wasn't such a damn chauvinist.

So I did some shopping and tried to relax. I'd called into the bank and told them to give the auditor access to whatever he needed. I knew it wouldn't go over well but the auditor, Martin I guess his name was, would get over it. Still, I couldn't help but worry.

So I set my sights on meeting up with Chris. It was almost 2 PM and I knew right where he would be. Buying around for his buddies so I headed over to the bar.

Sure enough his truck with outside. It wasn't two seconds inside the bar that I heard Chris and his buddies yelling various insults at each other as they played darts. Chris had been some sort of a dart champion at college so he likes to gloat about how good he was and people would take bets how big the spread was against the people he was playing.

"Are you looking this jackass when again?" I said as I walked up. Chris's attention immediately snapped me.

"Letting me hell I'm going easy on them and gave them a few points to start. You want in on the action five dollars a point on the spread." He said. "Unless, of course, you think I'm taken advantage of them."

"Look Chris, I'm sorry about those comments I made. It's just this audit and…" I stopped short when Chris grabbed me and pulled me to him. Anything that looked like an apology or sincere moment seem to be a call to action for him to touch me.

"There is enough blame to go around, So what you said you had me go and have a private party? Make it up to each other," he said. Oh, brother, I thought as I pushed myself away from him again. He was as refined as a dirty rock.

Just then there was a voice from behind me. "This guy bothering you?"

It was that guy Martin, and I'm not sure if he was trying to be funny or seriously thought that I couldn't handle Chris. But it attracted Chris's attention immediately. And I knew that wasn't good.

Jackasses being what they are, they did, in fact, pretty rowdy especially after their second round of beers. They started to pinch the ass of the bartender when she gets the bottles. She got mad at them and one of them tossed a bottle at the fireplace and broke it. "Hey, I got a return those for the deposit. You Ass!"

"You just go ahead and add that to my tab honey," said that guy Chris. "And while she brings us another round"

That was just great; all those guys needed was more alcohol. I noticed though that Chris really didn't drink. I know his type, he can work a crowd brings beads the natives but he's working an angle. Sort of like a politician trying to keep his people happy. It seemed like he was pretty simple to keep his people happy.

Just then I saw Ellis walk into the bar and headed over to Chris. Not sure what he said but pulling her to him did not seem to set well. So, of course, I do the stupid thing and butted in.

"This guy bothering you?" I said hoping once again to be charming and light but I guess it came out wrong because Chris put Elyse aside and stood up. He must've been 6'5"

"What did you say? What you fuck off city boy before I flick you out here."

"I don't know, seems like a public place so unless you're the owner I got a right to be here. It doesn't look like the lady really wanted you manhandling her."

"What you gonna do about it, I noticed you you little girly man orders the froufrou drinks like the ladies."

He was trying to get under my skin, not very original I had sort of expected it. And smart money said don't poke the bear but I've never been accused of being smart when it comes to dealing with amped-up guys in the bar.

"What? You tell me to step outside ncxt so we can settle this," I said.

"Goddamnit, you to stop!" Ellis said.

"You stay out of this. City boy needs a lesson in dance."

Here we go. Hadn't really thought this through, after all, there were seven but I hope there was some honor among these thieves and would just be me and him.

"Really, so should I lead or will you?"

"I want to beat your ass so hard," Chris said.

Whatever was going to happen had to happen quickly because the bartender was already on the phone. The other six backed off so at least that confirmed it would just be him. I guess he decided to lead as he swung and leaned on one side. I guess I forgot to mention that I study Aikido. I'm more of a lover, not a fighter but when you're lover you often piss off a lot of fighters who think their girl is their property. I got my ass kicked quite a few times in college and so I decided to take three years of martial arts elective.

I'm not much one for punching or kicking. I wasn't into grappling either so that just left a Kido. Which is the art of using another's momentum against them so I grabbed his wrist and flung them across the room through a couple of tables.

"Holy shit, did you see him throw Chris by his wrist."

Not the comment I wanted to hear because it generally comes right before six guys try to help out there buddy. Within a second three more were thrown and Chris was back. Another punch and again I sent him flying, this time against the bar.

"Come on you chickenshit fight," Chris spat.

"I am, this is how girly men with froufrou drinks fight. Maybe you would just like to calm down."

Chris was about to take another swing when the familiar sound of a shotgun racking a load could be heard and they all stopped.

"Shares going to be here in five minutes. But if you keep going I would be shooting someone in the ass in one. Time to go home," the bartender said. She didn't look like she was kidding. So I put my hands up and walk backward drank the last of my drink and left.

+Ellis

I couldn't believe what I was seeing; Martin must've been all of 5 feet six maybe and was fronting off Chris. He either had a gun or he knew how to fight because Chris is big and mean there are not a whole load people who will just stand up to him in a fair fight.

I yelled for them to stop and of course, it became a dick size contest.

All I could do is stand back near the bar with the bartender and hope no one got seriously hurt. I think she and I were both surprised when it turned into a Jackie Chan movie. Nobody could lend a punch on Martin. But I was equally impressed that Martin didn't actually hit anyone either. He just threw them around like rag dolls. Finally, the bartender had enough called the Sheriff and got out her shotgun.

Martin was first to back out of the bar but I knew that was just going to take it onto the street. So I stepped in.

"Don't even think it, Chris! You go to your truck and go home or you stay put."

"What? I can have some idiot disrespecting me like that."

"First of all your both idiots, and second of all yes you can. He's auditing the bank, and all I need is more trouble. You want those seed loans or do you want the bank shut down because he looks a little too close at some bullshit paperwork that got done eight years ago that isn't right? I'll handle him to use and give you any more trouble."

It did not sit well with Chris. His ego was as bruised as his ass but he backed down and told his friends to help pick up chairs and set tables back upright. By the time the Sheriff showed up, there was no sign of a commotion. Chris being Chris invited him to a drink when he got off duty. Everyone was friends again. I couldn't wait for Tuesday.

#

Wednesday

+Martin

But Tuesday Jen looked a little better. She got a little and got some day quill from the drugstore and pulled out her cameras and computer. The first place I found her was at the damn trashcan checking the lock.

"What are you doing?"

"I told you the first place I was up to was to check out this trashcan. I wasn't kidding," she said. She took a few pictures and then swiveled the lock open. "See, told you."

We looked inside and sure enough, it was full of papers. Jen dutifully climbed in and started browsing to see if any of it was confidential. This was probably going to take her most of an hour before she was satisfied.

"Well I'm heading over to the diner, you want me to bring you something?"

"No I don't eat breakfast," she said.

"Could've fooled me you wiped out the chicken," I said.

"I eat when I'm sick. Pretty much continuously. It's the only time I can get away with it and not gain any weight," she said taking a few snapshots of paper she found.

She was definitely odd. So I went to the diner ordered the same breakfast because it was pretty much the

45

only breakfast they had and I didn't like grits. The taller very thin man came over with a box of papers.

"You must be Leonard?"

"I am. My wife says to bring you these papers, do I need to be here? I got a couple of jobs. Got a drive to them because the tractor can't come to me and I need to rent a compressor before they run out they only got the one. Everything is there everything IRS boys got anyway. And some new stuff too."

"This should be fine, do you rent tools a lot?"

"Fair amount I guess. Don't really rent them my brother owns the place and I check it out."

"Do you give him anything in return? And does he have a record of what you check out? "

"Course it does. He needs your tracker where his stuff is. And yeah, I work on his machines and vehicles for free."

"While you invite your brother over tomorrow for breakfast I think I have an idea on how to lower your taxes. Maybe for both of you."

I finished eating my breakfast and headed to the bank I could not wait to have to face Ellis after that bar fiasco yesterday. And I can hardly wait for her to hear from John about the open trashcan.

+++

As expected the gang at the bank had heard everything about the bar scene. But the loan officer had also heard about Leonard and his tax needs. Not that help me any because it seems that she did his taxes and now looked at me like I was an IRS auditor.

At least I get to go into the vault today and get to the bottom of all this paper. The paper assets were the hardest part of the job and that's why hated small banks in small places. I would probably be combing through them all the way till Saturday. That is if I didn't get any help from the bank. But at 10 Ellis rolled in and I wanted to get right to business. Unfortunately, she didn't.

"What was that in the bar yesterday?"

"I don't really want to discuss this. Besides I went easy on him. You'll recall I didn't throw the first punch."

"No, but you certainly egged them on."

"And you didn't do much about it. Get your rocks off and watching her boyfriend protect your honor or whatever that was when he was mauling you."

She was fuming and I still had work to do. So I picked up my computer and headed to where I thought the stairs to the vault would be. I turned around and looked at her. Pretty sexy when she was mad. "We can do this all day or you get to work. You never see it my way and I'm not going to see it yours. At the end of the day, the FDC doesn't give a shit nor does the banking commission."

"You just stay away from that bar."

"I will go where I want and as you can see I'm not easy to intimidate so let's get to the vault and see what we can find shall we."

We worked and got through half of the papers which is further than I expected to get but Ellis helped out and she knew where everything was like the back of her hand. Jen never did come in. And when I left for the day I found out why. After she had finished with the can she found she was a little too weak to keep going. So she locked it up and went to bed.

+Ellis

Martin was blazing fast couldn't believe how quick he could add numbers in his head look at papers and determine their relevance within a second to things he'd never seen before. I heard from one of the girls who heard from the bartender who heard from the waitress at the diner that Martin was helping with Leonard's taxes. As far as the diner was concerned Martin was covered in gold.

He was an animal when it came to working and didn't stop for anything. I eat my lunch downstairs in the vault watching him. It was kind of sexy. I was the nerd in college studying economy and banking so I didn't get out much. Not that I wanted to because most of the other students really didn't get why I like the economy. It seemed like a lot of the other students just took it to be taking a major but really majored in partying. I never met someone into this stuff like I was. It seemed like Martin had a little of everything. If only he were so short.

# #
Wednesday

On Wednesday I met with Leonard and his brother and explained that they needed to start to create receipts for each other and charge the going rate for the tools. I explained that I knew he didn't actually have any money but the receipt would show he owed it. Since it was a tool rental for his business he could write most of that expense off. By the time I had gone back through five years of returns, I found about $200 that they owed him. When I looked at his actual forms he filed taxes single and I found out he and his wife were not actually married. That made him and his kids head of the household which is basically just a wealth redistribution scheme federal government came up with, they owed him almost $3000 a year.

I called a tax accountant I knew up in Chicago and sent him some papers and numbers. He pulled the old returns and refiled them all. It was about 1030 and I was late by the time I got done. Ellis came looking for me.

"Taking the day off?" Ellis asked.

"No, finishing up here. Be right there."

Just then Mabel came up and warmed up my coffee. "Honey," she referred to Ellis. "Is it just fabulous Martin found a $15,000 mistake the IRS made. If I had half a mind I'd take up with him." She winked at Elyse.

To which Ellis blushed a little. We spent the rest of the day in the vault and finished up the papers.

+Ellis

Martin was checking me out half the day. And I was thinking that a little more was going on with us than just numbers. I started to think that maybe he was a kinder spirit and I found myself fantasizing that he would be into me. But I knew all it was as a fantasy because how would I even approach him without everyone in town knowing and getting back to Chris. That was the subject that stuck out in my mind. I like Chris but he wasn't refined like Martin didn't seem to get me. It wasn't his fault he had his ways but I know he wouldn't understand the way Martin would. I started to feel conflicted and confused, I had only just met Martin and known Chris for years but suddenly felt like I need to make a choice between the two.

As tends to happen it got hot in the vault and I took off my coat. It was amazing we worked so well together that we finished gathering most of the data by the end of the day. Although it had been a long day.

"Well, that's it. That's all a paper the rest are all electronic. I can show you those tomorrow," I said.

"Cool."

"You know we should celebrate. Pretty sure you were kidding but you offered me a beer."

"Well, you'd have to go to my trailer; what would people say. Especially your boyfriend." Martin said.

"Well I did date Chris for a while but he's not my boyfriend."

"You guys taking a break?"

51

Fair enough he was feeling around the edges trying to determine what my motivation was. I wasn't sure myself.

"No, he's just a client now. And I'm sure would be fine after all you've got your little computer person in the trailer. Not like anything can happen."

"Well, I'm not sure the town would think of it like that. Big city boy with two women in this trailer. I can hear the scandal now," Martin said.

"You'd like that wouldn't you?"

"A three-way or scandal. Who am I kidding, of course, I would. But you're wound too tight I don't think you can handle it. Judging by the way you handle Chris anyway."

"What's that supposed to mean, handle Chris? There's nothing to handle," I said. "And I'm not wound tight, I can be pretty loose what I want to be."

"Really when you last time old Kitty was out for a spin?"

"What? You're a pig."

"Yeah, well, most of the other night was your fault. Why are you acting like you're some victim you have all the power."

"Maybe in some liberated town like Chicago but we are out here and things are a little simpler."

"Been in the same everywhere. We want the same things. There is not much mystery to how we work. Kind of like a dog. It gets confused when it's given too much control."

I wasn't sure what to say but I wanted him to be wrong and I wanted to find some fault in how he approached it. But it took me a little while to decide whether this was a misogynistic or feminist idea.

"So you're saying women have all the power?" I asked.

"I do. For example, right now you could get me to do just about anything. All you have to do is say yes." Martin said.

"Really? And what would I be saying yes to?" I said, a little curious and starting to feel a lot more warmth.

"You know that I'm talking about, you're the one standing there with her nipples poking through your shirt. You're a little hot and bothered and I gathered as much when you took off your coat and started checking me out," Martin said.

We were pretty close now and he wasn't wrong I was being drawn into the forbidden fruit of a man I didn't know but wanted to. This wasn't like me at all, I didn't do these kinds of things. I didn't go picking up men at bars or hook up, so why was Martin getting under my skin so deeply. I think we were about to kiss but then a tiny alarm went off. Shit, it was six.

"What's that?" Martin asked looking around. "Are we being robbed?"

"Shit, no. It's the fucking vault door giving us a 15-second warning that it's about the lock it's on a timer."

"But it's open and it's not moving? How can it lock us in?"

"But the big vault door the steel door up on top of the stairs," I said and ran for it.

I didn't make it I could hear the bolt click hard and we were locked in.

"Goddammit, this is just great. We are locked in until 6:00"

"that doesn't sound too bad," Martin said.

"That's when the loan officer comes in."

"Oh OK. No big deal I'll just call Jen and she can come to open it for us there's an overriding right?"

"Well, no not really."

"It's either yes or no question. And given vault security, it better be a yes or Jen's gonna write you up."

"Are you goddamn serious right now. We're stuck in here and you're still auditing me."

"See, told you that your wound is too tight," his hands caressing one of my breasts says he kissed me.

"Look at the bright side," he said breaking the kiss.

"What's the bright side?"

"No one sees you coming or going in the trailer."

+Martin

Getting locked into the vault with the Ellis was not the plan. I was hoping for an actual night of sleep. And I think I might be getting whatever Jen had of course. But standing there at the steel gate with her locked deeply in a kiss and caressing her body it could've been worse.

"So tell me about all this control I have," she said.

"You don't sound like you believe me? I'm hurt," I said pretending to be wounded.

"It sounds a little like bullshit you say to get women to pull off their panties if you ask me."

"Well that's the problem with women, they drank the feminist Kool-Aid."

"Okay, now I know you're full of shit."

"No seriously think about all of the women you've known who had the most power and their families. Were they always these top executives. Were they regular housewives it's a sort of ruled the roost," I said

"I can't think of any."

"Not your mom? Or your grandmother?"

"Well my grandmother had my grandfather wrapped around her finger," she said.

"See that's my point in your grandmother of course lived in the feminist enlightened age right?" I asked.

"Well, no my grandmother was born in 1910. Okay, I see where you're going with this but that shit doesn't work anymore."

"Really? You don't think so?, I said and unzipped my fly and pulled out my cock. "Go ahead and touch it."

"What? No!"

"Why not you want to. I mean you just let me kiss you and touch your breast? Touch my cock."

"Well doesn't work that way you have to be proper."

"Who says. Really think about it who's making these rules."

The gears were turning but she just didn't want to admit that the reason for all of this was the rule she put in place either through her own morals or simple desire.

"And so why are those rules in place? Is it because you're too uptight? Or do I have to follow them because you are a reward if I do?"

She bit her lip and refused to answer but I could I'd gotten to her.

+Ellis

Martin had been feeding his line about how I was in charge. I will say I certainly didn't feel in charge over the years. Relationships seemed confusing and twisted even difficult but that's how they're supposed to be right. It takes work, that's what they say anyway. Frankly, relationships have taken so much work over the years that I can take them or leave them. Not that I didn't want one but it took so much out of me and usually ended up in disappointment.

Now Martin was telling me it was my fault. But a lot of what he said made sense. Still, if I acted that way I would be a slot, wouldn't I? Or at worst I'd get a reputation for being unapproachable.

"Okay smart ass," I said, as I got up on the small counter in the vault to take a seat. "Suppose you're right, and you're not, but just suppose. What you're saying is that all of the women's liberation and the suffrage is wrong. We should have stayed barefoot and pregnant in the kitchen."

He walked over to me and put his hands on my hips. "I'm not saying that all. Two different arguments, I just said you're in control and I'm right. I never said that women didn't deserve rights, shouldn't be able to do what they want."

"So is that it Martin, like to be told what to do. Are you a beta. I don't think any of this will work on someone like Chris."

"No, I don't think I'm a beta just because I want to please a woman. And your wrong, it will work even better on a guy like Chris. Look at what he does for approval. Buys rounds of drinks for example," said Martin. "He's all about approval. He's not only seeking it, but he's also controlled by it."

Chris carried a lot of investments, seed loans, livestock, farm equipment. All for the people who worked his land. Could Martin be right? The scales were tipping toward Chris again. Now I was really confused.

"What would you do to please me?"

He reached under my skirt and pulled at my underwear. I lifted my butt a little and let him. This was crazy. But I didn't want to stop. He pushed my skirt up around my waist and without a seconds hesitation went down on me. I spread my legs wide to give him full access. It had been so long since a guy sucked my clit.

"Fuck, that feels so good," I said and ran my fingers through his hair.

"Mmmm, Like that," I purred as he put his tongue in my hole and rubbed my clit with his thumb. He was all in. I took my blouse off and pulled off my bra. I was close and I wanted more than anything to come on his mouth but I was on fire now and what I really wanted is a cock inside me. So I pushed him back. I loved that he didn't want to stop. "Fuck me."

His cock was still out and hard as a fireplace poker. The counting table I was on was low to the ground and I found out his cock at full mast was a lot bigger than I thought. Bigger than anyone else I had been with. I have to admit though it was a short list. I was ready when he slipped inside me.

58

"Jesus you huge," I told him, and he started to fuck me slow and deep. "Shit. I'm going to come."

The combination of his kissing my neck, that slow grind and my holding my leg up for him was too much. I couldn't hold back, an orgasm built up and waves of pleasure cascaded through me. I rubbed my clit a little to extend the sensations until it was too sensitive. It was a sort of a record for me. To come so easily and quickly. This was a slow marathon to Martin, not a race. But if it had been I finished first, and that was something rare in my sex life.

Martin took his time. I rode him for a while until I had a second orgasm and could not hold myself up anymore. He bent me over and took me from behind. I was maddeningly close again after his fucking me a few minutes and I finally reached under to my clit again and brought myself to a third orgasm. Fuck, was he ever going to come? I was getting the fucking of my life, it had to be a good forty minutes or an hour. I lost track.

I never thought I would say it but out it came. "I have to stop. I have to stop. God, you feel good but I can't take anymore."

"That's what I like to hear."

"Let me take care of you," I told him and got on my knees. I tried to get him in my mouth but I could barely get the head in. So I jacked him off with both hands as I licked the head. He leaned back and I watched him as he closed his eyes in concentration.

"I'm coming," he said. This was normally my queue to get out of the way but I found myself wanting to stay. The first blast of come went in my mouth, so did the second and I had to swallow, half had already run down my chin and onto my tits. The third blast hit my cheek as I turned away from this fire hose of jizz.

I started to giggle and let the rest of his come land on my tits. "Fuck, been a while. That's was quite a load."

"Just since last Saturday morning," Martin said a little too proud of himself. I Stood up and without hesitation, he french kissed me. Wow. now that was a first and it was so sexy that way he didn't care. He just wanted to kiss me.

+Martin

We got dressed and she was all smiling. It was hot and she was a beautiful woman but the aftermath of good sex came suck. Especially if this was the first time they get to feel like this. I didn't nip this in the bud, there would be the talk of meeting friends and the color of the centerpieces she likes at her wedding. But in the afterglow of the event, it was not the time to bring it up. So I was glad when she did.

"That was amazing. But that had more to do with you as a lover than any control I had," she said.

"I'm an amazing lover because I am trying to meet your expectations. I'm not masturbating here. Any guy will do it. If you tell him that's what you want. And tell him if you don't get it, he's done."

"Wow. I would have to be a bitch of a n'th degree to come out and tell a guy, make me come or hit the bricks."

"You don't have to be a bitch about it."

We had just gotten our clothes on and the last few kisses in when the little alarm sounded and the lock on the gate made a loud click.

"Jesus, How long did you fuck me?" Ellis asked and put her hand over her mouth.

"Hello? Is anyone down there. Hello?"

"Oh shit, Sally. The loan officer," Ellis said. "Yeah, Sally we are down here. Thank god you came back."

Someone was walking down the stairs and we tried to act casual, but we were failing.

61

"Well, the app said there was motion in the Vault and it was after closing. So I thought I would come to check it out. We are supposed to call the Sheriff I know but I was right here."

Sally, appeared and eyed the two of us for a second.

"Well, thanks. We appreciate it, I thought we would have to sleep down here."

"Well, that would have been a mess. Where would you have gone to the bathroom?"

Now that she said that I needed to pee. So I headed for the bathroom.

I thought about it on the toilet and wondered about the app Sally was talking about. When I got out I went down to get my computer and sure enough. Cameras. Wow. OK, that was a real problem. I was going to have to talk to Jen and see what she could do or this audit was null and void. I didn't tell Ellis, no need to make her freak out.

#

The next morning

I woke up to Jen making breakfast. She looked a lot better. She was still just dressed in a t-shirt and booty socks again, but the shirt was higher and he ass was plain to see.

"Wow, breakfast and a show?"

"Nothing you haven't seen before?"

"I've seen a woman ass before, sure. But this is a new side of you I haven't seen. At least not so graphically."

"What about Florida?"

"What about it?"

"Well, I woke up naked in your bed, after, you know?"

"What? No, I went out and ended up hooking up with some chick I met. You were so blitzed, I had to haul you out of there and get you to bed. I didn't undress you though. You did that at some point."

"But you were there getting dressed when I woke up," She said confused.

"I showered and was getting dressed, sure. But. Wait you thought all this time we had sex? Jen, I."

She looked really embarrassed now and pulled down her shirt and retreated to her bedroom and slammed the door. Shit. Now was not the time to ask her for any favors. Part of me was a little pissed off though. That she would think I took advantage of her. She had to know that she was like a sister to me. That I wouldn't do that.

I got up and finished the eggs and bacon she was cooking.

"Your food is done." And then I saw the two plates on the table. Great. She was making me breakfast. But as luck would have it there was a knock on the door. And it was Ellis, so why not make my problems worse. I opened the door to see if she would meet me somewhere.

"We have a problem," Ellis said and barged in.

"Welcome, come right in."

"What? Now you're modest?" she said and looked upset.

"I do have a roommate."

"I thought about it and the vault has a camera. Oh, I am so fucked," she said.

"I was going to talk to Jen about that this morning. I thought of the same thing."

Ellis sat down.

"Talk to me all you want, but she's right, you're fucked," Jen said sporting one of my sweat pants. How or why she had them I would find out later.

"Why?"

"It's a new system, got installed about six months ago. There's an on-site tape, but it's a black box buffer, all the video is streamed out on high speed and stored off-site at the main data center," she said.

"Can you get the data somehow?" I asked.

"That would take an act of God. Good thing you know one," she said. "I can't get the tape but I might be able to override it as a glitch. Mess with the time stamp on a loop of the right length. But I have to know the minimum time and when to start."

"Well, when we got stuck in the vaults was what? 6 and then the loan officer came back at about 7:30 or so," Ellis said.

"What? Ok, we are back to being screwed again," Jen said.

"Why?"

"Because the loan officer knows you were down there and so I can't just put on dead air. You guys have to be in the shot, doing shit that people do when they are trapped in a vault. Let me ask you this? Did she catch you?"

"What? Catch us?" Ellis tried not to look at Jen and turned red as a beet.

"No, she didn't we had finished fooling around by then," I told her.

"Ok, we record you in the vault sitting there for an hour and a half."

"How would we do that?" Ellis asked.

"Shut the back down for a physical audit. We have done it before. I'll be poking around and I turn alarms off and on, poke around. It won't be secure while I do it. It's not required for this audit because all the systems are so new and were already certified by the company. But I can be thorough and ignore that," Jen said. "After you two need to disappear. And Martin, you sign off as a consultant, you're no longer considered as independent. If you sign you could get into big trouble and lose your license. Donald has to sign the report."

"I know, ok, we can get him to do that. Tell him I'm sick and can't complete," I said.

"Ok, I'll call him."

The plan in place, it was a simple matter of going in and working in the vault. Jen did her magic and we finished the report, all but the final walk-through and signatures. Jen also added her report, with a healthy number of minor violations. Her premise on this was that they would focus less on the financials and more on the security. But she was punishing me, but I deserved it, thinking with my dick. While Jen finished up we went for a walk.

"Hungry?" I asked her.

"Yeah. I could eat."

Mable floated over and set down some cups. "Well, look at you two. Have a nice night?"

"What?" Ellis asked.

"Well, word has it you two got locked into the vault," Mable winked. Ellis cannot control that damn blushing.

"Yeah. Locked us in for a few minutes," I said.

"That's all it takes around my house," she said and took our order.

+Ellis

Martin and I are realists I think. It was great and I can still feel him in me. But this is going nowhere. But a thoughtless moment might cost me my job. Now it's all over town that we were locked in and we could have been playing chess down there and the rumors would still fly. Still, I'm glad it happened. I wished I could have that feeling again. But after what Martin said about Chris, I wished it could be with him. All night I lay there with a mixture of terror, guilt, and excitement. Now that I knew how it could be, I wanted to know how to get that. Martin seems to think all men are the same.

"So, I wanted to ask you something," I asked.

"Shoot," Martin said.

"I don't want you to take this the wrong way. But, how do I get Chris to do that for me?"

He smiled and sat back. "Really."

"I mean not that I don't like you or anything."

"No, I get it. Thank God."

"What?"

"I was hoping you would feel that way, sort of. You're great I am sure but I'm not moving here and I suspect you like your job too."

"And I don't love you," I said.

"Yeah, and there's that. But I think I can help you out. I've actually done this a couple of times. As I said, he already wants to, he just doesn't know it yet," Martin said. I smiled as Martin laid out his plan. The first part of it was dinner and let Chris know I was going out. That was easy. I just let Mabel overhear us making the plan to go to a fancy restaurant on Friday and threw in Chris as a concern.

Friday

Audits are always exciting to me. I have to say there is no better feeling. I love it. But this one has been a little more exciting than I wanted. We gave Don a line about his needing to review because of his expertise. Jen was not speaking to me. And I was out on Friday with a woman looking to turn a boyfriend into something more.

"So do you think he will show?" I asked Ellis.

"Pretty sure. I told his brother just to stir the pot. I hope he does not go off. Worse yet, write me off," she said.

We were into a salad when he showed and towered over the table.

"So, this is it then. This is how it's going to be?" he said.

"Look," I told him.

"You shut your fucking mouth," he spat at me. Showtime. I thought I would have to prompt her but she went into action.

"Sit the fuck down Chris. Your embarrassing me?"

"Not till I have said what a came for," He said. Then she surprised even me.

She got up, got on the chair and started at him, loud too.

"I said sit the fuck down you are embarrassing me god damn it. I don't give a flying pigs fuck what you have to say. I'm done listening. Sit down," she demanded and the whole place looked at him. Small town, that has got to travel fast. I tried not the smile.

"Now. I can guess what you want to know. So here it is. I fucked Martin, and it was good. I loved it and I came three times. I had to tell him to stop I was out of my mind with pleasure. He made me understand I deserve more," She told him.

"I don't need to hear this. Why are you humiliating me," he said in that Sam Elliot low growl tone. He just wanted to be quiet now.

"Oh, it's about you? No, It's about me. And yes you need to hear it. You know what, I don't owe you a thing. We broke up and it was my fault," She said.

"No. It wasn't your fault. I know I can be an ass," He said.

"No. Your just a dog that doesn't know your place. I remember your mother, she never let your dad get away with the way you acted. He wasn't an ass, and neither are you."

He perked up a little and it looked like he caught on there was hope.

"Now, we can do this a couple of ways. We can go home, all three of us and Martin can teach you how to screw me," He did not like that at all. "or you can just take me home and we can talk about what I want out of this. You're a good man, but you have no idea what I need because I didn't tell you. And Chris, you're going to need to go downtown, if get my meaning and take care of me first."

"I can do that. I thought you thought it was gross. I didn't think you liked oral," he said.

"I like it a lot. But I get why you think that I haven't been as enthusiastic as I could be. But then ten minutes does not really charge me up. Ok."

"OK, Let's talk. Your place."

"No. Take me home, the ranch. Ok."

He nodded and smiled at her. She smiled back.

"Enjoy dinner Martin."

"Have a good weekend Ellis," I said.

I had them pack up the two dinners to go. Jen deserved more after asking her to do what she did. Man, what a week.

I made my way back to the RV. I will be glad to get back to Chicago and relax a while. I thought it was a quiet town, but the drama is too much for me. I guess you learn to be disconnected in the crowd.

When I reached for the handle of the RV I heard a soft low moan. Jen? So I peeked. Yes, an asshole thing to do but there she was, knees up rubbing one out. She was watching a video on her computer. She was pretty sexy, kinky too. She had two in her hole and with the other hand, she had another up her butt. I was getting a hard-on. So another asshole move deserves another. I opened the door and started to get in.

She, of course, jumped up and slammed the laptop shut. "I thought you were at dinner."

"Yeah, Apparently," I said. "I brought it back for you. Ellis made up with the cowboy and so I thought you might like hers. Salmon? Or would you rather have steak."

"Salmon is good." She was still mortified and bunched up on her chair.

"What are you watching?" I asked.

"Um, well."

"You don't have to tell me. It's OK. Eat. It's been a hell of a week. Beats Florida by a mile."

She opened the laptop and showed me the video.

"Oh. I see. I thought you couldn't recover the video? Pretty good quality, Grey does nothing for me."

"Line 10 on the report."

"I didn't read it, Donald is handling it, remember?"

"Buffer fault. The company that installed it didn't initialize the interface to the FTP. So it had about 48 hours of video on it and nothing had uploaded. I called them and they gave me the codes I needed to wipe it. But I saved a copy before I did," she said.

"Why?"

"So now I have a video of you like you have of me."

"I can throw it out."

"Yeah, but you can't unsee it. And besides, I kind of wanted there to be a Florida," She said.

"Really?"

"You know why I didn't in Florida right?"

"No. Why?"

"Because you were drunk. That's all."

"Really?" she said quietly.

"Really."

We sat there and she uncurled a little as the video played. I looked at her.

"Want to make a new video?" I asked.

She nodded.

"Promise not to fall in love?"

"No."

I moved over to her side and kissed her. "Thanks for saving my ass."

"Yeah. Now you owe me!"

"How do you want to start?"

"Looks like you're really good at eating pussy, let's start there."

We decided to take a vacation and took the RV to Jens home town. She was right what a hole. We made a few movies and had some fun. It was fun and I gave her some pointers how to get with this guy Dillon in the data analysis group. What can I say? Always a bridesmaid. But I could have a worse fuck buddy.

I got an email from Mrs. Franklin. Apparently she gushed about how dedicated I was and advised the folks in New York that they needed to promote me. So that might be happening. I'm sure Dick is not all that happy. God knows what she told him, but I am sure it made him crazy. I might stay in Chicago, might go to New York. Who knows.